Dear Parents and Educators,

Welcome to Penguin Young Readers! As parents and educators, you know that each child develops at his or her own pace—in terms of speech, critical thinking, and, of course, reading. Penguin Young Readers recognizes this fact. As a result, each Penguin Young Readers book is assigned a traditional easy-to-read level (1–4) as well as a Guided Reading Level (A–P). Both of these systems will help you choose the right book for your child. Please refer to the back of each book for specific leveling information. Penguin Young Readers features esteemed authors and illustrators, stories about favorite characters, fascinating nonfiction, and more!

Pal and Sal

LEVEL **2**

GUIDED READING LEVEL **E**

This book is perfect for a **Progressing Reader** who:
- can figure out unknown words by using picture and context clues;
- can recognize beginning, middle, and ending sounds;
- can make and confirm predictions about what will happen in the text; and
- can distinguish between fiction and nonfiction.

Here are some **activities** you can do during and after reading this book:
- Rhyming Words: The names Pal and Sal rhyme—they are words that sound the same. On a separate sheet of paper, make a list of words that rhyme. See how many you can come up with!
- Make Connections: Pal is all alone in the beginning of the story. How does this make him feel? Think about a time when you have been all alone, too. How did this make you feel?
- Retelling: What happened in this story? Retell it from the beginning.

Remember, sharing the love of reading with a child is the best gift you can give!

—Bonnie Bader, EdM
  Penguin Young Readers program

*Penguin Young Readers are leveled by independent reviewers applying the standards developed by Irene Fountas and Gay Su Pinnell in *Matching Books to Readers: Using Leveled Books in Guided Reading*, Heinemann, 1999.

For my pal, Betina—RAH

For my daughter Paris
and my friend Ronnie—BO

Penguin Young Readers
Published by the Penguin Group
Penguin Group (USA) Inc., 375 Hudson Street, New York, New York 10014, USA
Penguin Group (Canada), 90 Eglinton Avenue East, Suite 700, Toronto, Ontario M4P 2Y3, Canada
(a division of Pearson Penguin Canada Inc.)
Penguin Books Ltd., 80 Strand, London WC2R 0RL, England
Penguin Group Ireland, 25 St. Stephen's Green, Dublin 2, Ireland (a division of Penguin Books Ltd.)
Penguin Group (Australia), 250 Camberwell Road, Camberwell, Victoria 3124, Australia
(a division of Pearson Australia Group Pty. Ltd.)
Penguin Books India Pvt. Ltd., 11 Community Centre, Panchsheel Park, New Delhi—110 017, India
Penguin Group (NZ), 67 Apollo Drive, Rosedale, Auckland 0632, New Zealand
(a division of Pearson New Zealand Ltd.)
Penguin Books (South Africa) (Pty.) Ltd., 24 Sturdee Avenue,
Rosebank, Johannesburg 2196, South Africa

Penguin Books Ltd., Registered Offices: 80 Strand, London WC2R 0RL, England

Text copyright © 1998 by Ronnie Ann Herman. Illustrations copyright © 1998 by Betina Ogden.
All rights reserved. First published in 1998 by Grosset & Dunlap, an imprint of Penguin Group (USA)
Inc. Published in 2011 by Penguin Young Readers, an imprint of Penguin Group (USA) Inc.,
345 Hudson Street, New York, New York 10014. Manufactured in China.

Library of Congress Control Number: 97027174

ISBN 978-0-448-41716-5   10 9 8 7 6 5 4

PENGUIN YOUNG READERS

LEVEL
PROGRESSING
READER
2

PAL AND SAL

by R. A. Herman
illustrated by Betina Ogden

Penguin Young Readers
An Imprint of Penguin Group (USA) Inc.

Pal is the littlest pony
at the Star Ranch.
All the big horses
are too busy to play.

So Pal runs in the field alone.

He jumps over logs alone.

He swims in the pond alone.

It is not much fun.

Pal wants a friend to play with.

Billy has come to live

on the ranch.

His dad is a cowboy.

One day,

Billy rides Pal

to school.

When they get there,

Billy leaves Pal in the field.

"Be good," Billy says to Pal.

"Wait for me here."

Pal waits.

He nibbles some grass.

He swishes his tail.

He tries to be good.

But there is nothing to do.

So Pal trots over to a window
and peeks in.

There is Billy.

And there are Billy's friends.

Pal wants a friend, too.

The children see Pal.

"Look!" they say.

"Pal wants to come to school!"

But the teacher says,

"School is for children—

not for ponies."

She takes Pal back to the field.

"Stay here, Pal," she says.

The next day,

Billy rides Pal to school again.

This time there is a surprise

for Pal.

"Look, Pal!" says Billy.

"Kate rode Sal to school, too!"

Now Pal and Sal

run in the field together.

They nibble grass together.

They swish their tails together.

Nibble, nibble.

Swish, swish.

After school,

Kate goes home with Billy.

Billy and Kate play together . . .

. . . and so do Pal and Sal.

They jump over logs.

They swim in the pond.

Pal is not alone anymore.

Pal has a pal!